A Battleaxe and a Metal Arm 3:

Over the Infinite Wall

Samuel Fleming

Cover Art by David Leahey

ISBN-13: 978-1-954679-09-2 (paperback)
ISBN-13: 978-1-954679-08-5 (ebook)

Thank you to my Beta Readers

and to my First Reader,

Mel.

Contents

Previously… vi

The Hall 1

The Wode 5

The Road 19

The Village 28

The Gatehouse 48

The Infinite Wall 67

Reset Again 73

Spoiler-Free excerpt from BAMA 4 ii

Thank you for Reading v

Connect with the Author iv

"It is easier to accept death
when one believes that they
will pass with purpose."
—*unknown*

Previously...

Death was not the end.

After their first death at the hands of the hydra, the elven spellweaver, Helesys Byyra, and her human barbarian comrade, Taunauk, found themselves in the same stone room from whence they started. They quickly realized that not only had they been reborn, they had retained the wolf-plate, and the dungeon had changed. There were two paths where before there was only one.

Again they took the left path and they saw no wormsign or flooding. Instead they came upon rooms full of scrap wood, scrap armor, scrap metal and an outcast goblin, named Widewill. The lone goblin told them of his old tribe that lived in the hallways up ahead and that they followed the god, Zhug. Widewill warned them not to cross Zhug and not to go into a place called the Crypt.

With little choice, Helesys and Taunauk pressed forward through the halls, weary of traps. All the while, the weaver felt they were being watched by some unseen, unknown force. They passed by a horde of goblins sleeping in stacks of old barrack beds. Just when the two were nearly passed, they were confronted by the battle-hardened goblin leader, Stizzai, who ordered them to go no further.

Neither side would back down and the resulting fight woke the horde. Taunauk's strength and cunning was barely a match for the speed and ferocity of Stizzai, and the two stayed locked in mortal combat while Helesys kept the horde at bay with shots from her wand-arm. Eventually the pair were overwhelmed and forced to retreat past Stizzai and further down the hall. Their escape was short lived and they found themselves surrounded on all sides by the goblin tribe and spoken to by the voice of Zhug—he would offer them no mercy!

So Helesys blasted a hole in the trapdoor in the middle of the room and the pair thought they had escaped, only to find themselves in the pitch-black confines of the Crypt. Again they ran for their lives, this time from the creeping monster that filled the cave. Both Helesys and Taunauk, had no idea the horrible fate that would've befallen them if they had perished to the Many-Handed Horror, Shomosk. They were only saved by another of the weaver's spells—come back to her in a time of need.

They found an exit from the Crypt, only to wind up face to face with Zhug's towering metal guardians. Both Taunauk and Helesys fought bravely, calling upon the deepest wells of their strength to tarnish—but not destroy—their attackers and so impress Zhug enough that the god granted them an audience.

At the ends of their strength they were brought before Zhug, who was not a god, but a giant and a mage of staggering size and intelligence. He had amassed enough gold and magic-imbued items to fill a room. It was there that Helesys and Taunauk learned that they were not the only beings damned to endless death and rebirth, but that other creatures could not bring back treasures such as they could. As a boon, Zhug granted them each one item from his treasure horde: Helesys chose a magekiller token and Taunauk chose an ironwood shield. Zhug asked only that if they managed to live and die enough times to return to his realm that they grant him mercy. Then the god of the goblins granted them a swift death.

Helesys and Taunauk again found themselves in that humble room. The elf confronted the barbarian about his near-death at the many hands of Shomosk. To which Taunauk replied that he would aspire to always "go first" into death—that he would not watch a friend die.

Questions upon questions heaped upon their shoulders. Chief of which: Why were Helesys and Taunauk able to bring back treasures after death when all others could not? Why were they different?

~ ~ ~

The Hall

Taunauk led the way down the dungeon hall with torch in hand. This time they had no choice of direction and followed the straight path for hours without end in sight. The grey stones were painfully familiar and darkness stretched out into a void in front and behind them.

Helesys had grown accustomed to the silence. In truth, she had not known what to say after their conversation upon this last rebirth, when Taunauk told her that he could not bear to see her die. His insistence that he always "go first" into death seemed both human and chauvinistic, and made the elf wonder whether he saw her as an equal or a female.

Helesys could not remember much about life before the dungeon—about the nations or races or cultures and customs—but she felt in her bones that a long-lived elf would not be so quick to lay down their life for another. It seemed to her that self-sacrifice was something that was noble to a short-lived race and impossibly foolish to a long-lived one.

Of course, there was always the possibility that Taunauk had remembered something else: Perhaps a debt he owed to

her and repaid in that fashion. ...They had been slow at revealing their family names to one another. It might follow that they
would be slow in revealing others.

She looked upon the outlander and reminded herself that
regardless of what they had been, they were comrades now.
Trapped in the same plight. Zhug, the self-proclaimed goblin
god, had told that he and many far more powerful and terrible
creatures were trapped in the endless cycle of death and rebirth. If Helesys and Taunauk did not trust each other, how
could they hope to succeed in escape when so many others had
failed? And so it was with the logic of necessity that Helesys
resolved to trust her comrade.

Besides, down here the concept of a long-life hardly seemed
to matter when death would put them back to square one, like
clearing a gameboard and resetting the pieces.

No. *Not square one*—that was the key difference.

The elf and the barbarian had brought back the wolf-plate.
Now they had brought back the barbarian's ironwood shield,
Everfall, and the sorceress's magekiller token, a coin stained
with the blood of a murdered weaver. The dark wood shield
covered the outlander's back while the magekiller token lay inside the arcane workings of the weaver's gauntlet. It was Zhug
who told them that they were different. That they alone could
bring back items after death—a trait shared with only a handful
of other dungeon myths. However the goblin king had ne-
glected to say *who* these myths were.

And so the elf and the human found themselves still wading
through mystery, one as long and seemingly as endless as the
impossible geometry of the hallway.

~

Hours stretched on in the endless hallway and Helesys could bare the silence no longer. "I think I was a warrior."

"That much is clear by your skill," Taunauk said.

"I mean to say, I think I was a soldier. When we fought in the flooded temple, the splashes of water reminded me of blastshells."

"I know not what you mean."

"Concentrated powder and fire and magic. Battlefield artillery. Bottled Death. Made for killing dozens and hundreds at a time."

"You remember this?"

"Like a dream. Echoes of a dream. I cannot remember more. Not yet."

Taunauk seemed to contemplate this as they walked, their footsteps alone amongst the silence.

Some minutes later he said, "I remember fields. Vast green fields. Warm sun. I feel that was home to me and my people. Is it strange to have emotion with no memory?"

"No," she responded quickly. *"The heart remembers quicker than the mind."* This was wisdom yet she could not remember the source.

The barbarian grunted in affirmation. "What do you feel when you remember the blastshells?"

Helesys had resolved to be open with her comrade, but in that moment she realized honesty would be a recurring vow. A vow of honesty with her comrade and with herself. One she would make anew with each revelation.

A vow that she made anew in the flickering torchlight of the hallway. With a trembling voice she replied, "When I think of the blastshells, I am terrified."

Taunauk paused and turned to her. "There is no shame in fear. It is known by the lowest animals and the most fierce. It is known by brutes and innocents, by assassins and kings. It is the language of the living." In spite of his reassurances, the torchlight cast harsh shadows upon his face.

"Before this is all through, I suspect we will know a great many things. Least of which will be fear," she replied. "The greatest of which will be the triumph of escape."

Taunauk smiled in the sharp light. "That spirit will carry us far."

~ ~ ~

The Wode

Helesys had lost track of time before they came to another landmark. The impossible hallway gave way to a forest. The barbarian and the elf were speechless as they stepped out onto dirt.

Taunauk knelt and grabbed a handful of soil, then brought it to his lips. *"Màthair talmhainn."*

It was night outside and the forest stretched out into the gloom. The trees rose up hundreds of feet into the heavens. Their thick trunks were bare and their branches congregated at the utmost tops. In spite of the dense canopy, the light of a full moon blazened through, casting the forest in a silvery light. The breeze carried with it the smell of grass and life.

If Helesys had seen such beauty before in her life, it could not have compared to the feeling of having stepped out into the open air after their time in the dungeon. The power of her wand-arm had brought the comfort of a candle in the darkness—stepping out into the forest was akin to a roaring fire.

Neither spoke for a long time as they basked in the sight. Though she almost asked it—she almost gave breath to the terrible question: *Do you think we're free?*

She turned to look at the exit, the hallway and the dungeon from whence they came. The entrance looked small against the stone face of the building. There was no torchlight to mark it and so it sat humbly in the wall, an ominous square amongst the stacked blocks—a silent scream that would be impossible to hear until it was too late. Until one was already within its impossible geometry.

The stone wall rose up and up, even higher than the giant trees of the forest. Helesys craned her head to try to see the top and nearly fell backward. It rose up so high that its blue-gray stone faded into blackness and blotted out the sky, giving the illusion of a starless night.

And with it came a shudder and a quiet whisper: *You will never be free. You will always look back and see the towering darkness from over the trees. Over the mountains. Across the world.*

"We must go forward," Taunauk said. Though he followed her eyes, he did not try to see the top as she had; he did not crane his head to look at madness.

Helesys nodded and turned toward purpose. The forest called to them. Lovely, dark and deep. A savior from the cold, familiar stone.

The forest stretched on. Taunauk had extinguished their torch and so they walked by the light of the moon. It would have been a beautiful night, if not for the specter of the dungeon towering behind them.

"Where do you think we are?" She asked.

Taunauk shrugged his massive shoulders. "I have no memory of this place."

Neither did she. More worrisome was that no more of her memory had returned. If they were truly free of the dungeon, would their memories suddenly return? Helesys turned to regard the dungeon from a distance but saw only the towering trees of the forest. The canopy blocked the horrid place from view. Would any amount of distance be far enough from it?

~

They walked and walked and night and the forest stretched on. Helesys's legs ached. All of the impossible hallways had not stretched on such as this. But it was Taunauk that suggested they stop for the night—that they save their strength.

She tried not to let too much gratitude show on her face.

Taunauk took first watch while Helesys slept on the sparse grass and soft ground. Slept and dreamt of never-ending stone, blind turns in the darkness.

When Taunauk woke her, time had passed all too quickly but it was still moonlit night in the forest. The barbarian fell asleep quickly and with a quiet snore, leaving Helesys alone in the night.

Her mind wandered. The elf tried to think of home but her memory was not merciful. In the silence, she burned the power of her gauntlet and the metal felt warm like a quiet fire. It was an odd thing, metal skin and arcane blood that she could feel through, that moved as if it were an extension of herself. It was familiar, yet so much of its potential was locked behind her memories. If she could only talk to it, maybe it would divulge the rest of its secrets. Helesys chuckled at the ridiculousness of the thought.

Some hours into her watch, fog rolled in. It came quick and heavy, and blotted out all but the closest trees. It brought a chill that woke Taunauk and the pair watched the eerie sight.

Then a strange creature walked through the trees, so tall that they could only see its slender limbs which disappeared up into the fog. It walked on five thin legs, saplings compared to the other trees. Each a ghostly gray hue as if they were made from the fog itself. Though its stride was lumbering, each leg struck the ground in utter silence—not even a tremor to mark their passing. Helesys envisioned a great spider walking, threading its way through the trees high above.

She watched both the creature and Taunauk, for the barbarian seemed to have a sense about these things, but he did not stir. He watched with the same wide wonder that she did.

The procession crossed only ten paces in front of them and lasted not even a minute before the thin legs disappeared into the fog. Helesys didn't breathe until after the sight was gone. The fog passed soon after, following the path of the creature.

"We should move," the outlander said.

Helesys agreed. "Did you sense anything from the creature or the mist?"

Taunauk shook his head. "Some things are.. Too far removed. I sensed no urgency about it, but that is all."

"Perhaps it wanders as we do."

"Perhaps."

The outlander's uncertainty was ominous but not unfounded. Helesys felt there would be a great many things they would encounter that would be as fleeting and as unknowable as the fog strider. There was Shomosk, the Many-Handed Horror of the goblin crypt, and the greatworm, the only trace of which they saw was an old borehole.

As the two wandered further into the night and the forest, Helesys said a silent prayer to a god that she did not remember. She prayed that the dungeon itself would not be counted amongst those unknowable things—that they would come to know it, understand it, and that their stay within would be short.

~

They went many more hours through the forest before finding signs of other life and the first they saw was more stone. They came upon a design of fist-sized stones, arranged to depict a crescent moon several paces across. Triangles were arranged in a circle around the crescent moon such that their points were facing out.

Both Helesys and Taunauk scanned the woods but saw no other signs.

"What do you think it means?" Helesys asked. "A crescent moon in front of the sun? Those triangles meant to be the sun's rays?"

The outlander only grunted in thought.

They walked further and found three more stone designs. Another of a moon. Two of a wolf face—the same pattern and shape as on the wolf-plate in Helesys's pocket. One of the three heads on the armor scrap from the goblin realm.

"We keep seeing this symbol," the elf said. "This cannot be coincidence."

"Agreed."

Taunauk's attention snapped to the right and in a blink his axe was in his hands. Deep in the gloom was a gray wolf, head high and still, regarding them. Helesys glanced around them and was met with a half dozen more wolves. Though the wolves were still and calm, they had the elf and human surrounded. Outnumbered.

"Refresh my memory outlander. Are wolves normally dangerous?"

"No."

The wolves stared back, patient, and the moment grew tense.

It seemed a shame to harm such beautiful creatures but if they attacked, the elf would not hesitate. It would be easy for her to deal with them as she did the fishmen and the hydra. She would not lose sleep over it.

But no such violence was needed, for the wolves walked off and disappeared behind trees. In their place, several brown robed figures reappeared. They walked around and gathered in front of Helesys and Taunauk. Only then did the barbarian rest the pommel of his axe on the ground and rest both hands on top of it. Only then did the weaver calm the frenzied power of her gauntlet.

Helesys looked upon their faces and saw a mix of human and elves. The tallest, a beautiful dark-haired elf stepped forward.

"Forgive our curiosity," he said with a disarming smile. "New travelers are few and far between through our woods."

"And are they often violent?" Helesys asked.

"Sometimes. You must admit you have the look about you. The look of capable violence."

"I'm afraid mirrors are few and far between," she replied.

At that, several of the robed figures smiled. One of the rose-cheeked women asked, "Will you stay here with us?"

Taunauk answered, "We ask for safe passage and safe passage, alone."

The woman asked, "Do you have no home?" To which others echoed, "*No home.*"

The lead elf waved a hand, "Silence. They are seekers." He turned back toward Helesys and Taunauk and shook his head. "You must forgive my family. They are every bit as young as they look. My name is Qinmarïs. You will have safe passage if that is what you want. You would also have a warm fire to rest beside and company for a while."

Helesys looked to her comrade and saw his steely eyes unwavering, hands still resting on the top of his axe. She rested a metal hand on his. "We do not always need to hurry toward the next death."

After a moment he grunted in reply.

~

They followed Qinmarïs and the others deeper into the woods, past more stone patterns of wolves, crescent moons and eclipses. Past sapling trees bent and grown in runic patterns. To half a dozen more robed figures gathered around a bonfire. Three danced around the pile and swung their robes as they did. The others chanted a song in a language unfamiliar.

Helesys wand-arm whirred with life and the song was transformed.

Qinmarïs bid them sit and Helesys wound up sitting between the robed leader and her comrade. Taunauk sat with his axe across his lap.

When the Fall has come and gone.
  The burrow's only just begun to warm
As snow falls and nights grow long.

> *Sleeping, drifting.*
> *Chase me around the den, Nuzzle my fur*
>   *This can't be happening*
> *When the woods are full with people*
>   *And wolves can't stop. Solemn howls.*
>   *Where are we?*
> *Something's wrong with the Wode.*

"It's the first song we all learn," Qinmaris said while the other druids continued singing. The voices lingered somewhere between human and a wolf's howl. "Though we have lived here long we have not forgotten that something is wrong with the forest."

Helesys asked, "Qinmaris, what is so special about the wolf?"

"The wolf is one of the noblest animals. One of the most revered."

Helesys reached within her pocket and pulled out the scrap of armor from Zhug's barracks. "We keep seeing the symbol of a wolf. We saw it in other realms too."

He looked over the armor piece, rubbing his thumb over the engraving. "There are stories but I never believed them. Matron Mildé said that wolves were the rulers of this place. That the line of the wolf goes back to the very beginning. I always thought they were stories. Perhaps not."

Helesys held out her normal hand and Qinmaris reluctantly gave back the armor piece. She placed it back in her pocket, beside the wolf-plate that she would not show.

"Thank you for that," he added. "Thank you for giving me back a bit of faith. How many deaths has it been?"

"Only two," Helesys replied.

"Isn't that enough?"

"Not enough to dissuade us."

Qinmarïs bowed his head. "I died nine times before I found these woods. Thankfully I do not remember much of them. Time has done me a kindness, in that respect."

Helesys sighed. "I have so many questions and denizens that speak common are few and far between. "

He chuckled. "We are druids. Open to all who seek to live in harmony with nature."

"How long have you been here?"

Qinmarïs looked up at the sky, or what little could be seen through the trees. "It's so hard to tell. The night is not perpetual here, though there is no true day. Sometimes the sky will turn to dusk—that is all. I have seen a sunrise only once. It was fleeting. Like the sun was scared and had forgotten what to do. It didn't even come over the wall."

Taunauk asked, "The wall?"

The beautiful elf saddened a bit. "I forget that you have not been here as long as I. The Wode—the forest—is great, but it is not endless. There is a wall around it that reaches up to the sky. A wall built so that none can ever leave."

Helesys and Taunauk shared a knowing glance. Eventually they would go to the wall.

She asked, "What of food and drink?"

"Hunting of course. As for water, there are streams. Even rain on occasion."

Something in his eyes told Helesys not to ask what game he spoke of. There were monsters trapped here and so likely there were deer or rodents… Of course there were people too.

"Matron Mildé is the elder?" Helesys asked, changing the subject.

He nodded. "She was here long before us and will be here long after us. She is the matron of the pack—of our clan. She may have more answers but she is notoriously obtuse."

~

The chanting and dancing stopped abruptly as another figure approached. Qinmariïs stood and whispered for Helesys and Taunauk to rise. All other druids bowed as she passed except for Qinmariïs.

Helesys found herself looking up to the figure, whom she guessed correctly was the matron. She walked in lumbering strides and loomed over the other druids, even Helesys and Taunauk. She was lanky, with knobby shoulders that appeared bulbous beneath her long robe. Her hands were clasped beneath the long sleeves, which fell loose over skinny forearms. The matron's face was elven and gaunt, her eyes yellow and hidden beneath deep brows. Shaggy grey hair hung out from the neck of her robe. Her lips were purple and black.

"And the babes shall be welcomed with open hearts and warm hearths by their lupine saviors," the matron said. Behind her, several druids nodded along in contemplation.

"We thank you for your hospitality," Helesys said and forced herself a shallow bow. Her wand arm hummed with silent power and apprehension. Beside her Taunauk stood tall, both hands gripping below the axehead.

Matron Mildé's hands flicked beneath her robe and she sneered, "*Restu senmova, šafidetoj.*" Helesys heard the words echo in her mind. *Be still, little lambs.*

Helesys felt her muscles grow taught where she stood. Though she tried to move, her muscles would not budge. They stayed flexed, pulling equally on one another. It was even hard to breathe as the muscles of her chest fought one another.

It felt as if the matron was breathing on her shoulder, close enough to touch even though she stood across from them. Warm, canine breath. Worse, Helesys could feel the wolf-mother's thoughts pressing against her own: *Little lambs. Lambs. Lambs.*

Taunauk had raised his axe to swing, but was frozen midway. He groaned in frustration.

Matron Mildé smiled, her purple-black lips bearing dagger-sharp teeth. "Do not despair. I will grant you a gift. The gift of a home. The gift of a pack." She turned and walked a short distance away, her bony shoulders spasming beneath her robe.

She slipped the hood off—hair hands skeleton-thin with long claws—and hair grey hair grew dense and down her neck to a full mane. Then she pulled the neck-string of her robe, letting it fall slack around her shoulders and then down to the ground. Her bones grew dense, her pale skin turned grey with thick fur.

Matron Mildé turned revealing a gaunt and spindly-muscled body. Her nose and mouth elongated into a half-snout— somewhere between elf and wolf. Her purple-black lips thinned, no longer hiding her canine teeth. She stood her full, towering height as a werewolf.

Qinmaris held up his hands, "Matron, I made a promise to them—"

"—Step back, lupeto." Her voice somewhere between a whisper and a wolf's growl. "This is my forest and you give no quarter that I cannot rightfully take."

The druids all around began to chant, "Mordu ilin. Mordu ilin kaj ili restos." *Bite them. Bite them and they will stay.* All except Qinmaris.

Unbeknownst to them, Helesys's metal arm whirred with silent life and deep within it she felt the magekiller token spinning its own enchanting whisper. It spoke to her in a language for which there were no words, the language of dripping blood, stuttered step, of a gasp caught midway in the throat. The dark and deadly calling of the token mixed with the raw arcane energy of her wand and coursed through her veins, negating the magic of the matron.

Helesys's muscles relaxed and her breathing slowed. Power hummed in her arm. The elf weaver smiled and this caused the matron much duress.

"What of you, elf?" she asked. The matron lowered herself to the ground, to a crouch. "What *sorcery* is this?"

"The kind that reminds other weavers they are still mortal," Helesys replied.

In spite of her boast, Taunauk was still frozen beside her. The other druids had ceased their chanting and glanced between her and the matron, unsure of what to do.

The matron snarled. "I should tear you asunder, but that would be a kindness. No—I will make you a wolf and spend eternity with your head between my claws."

"I will kill you and you will spend a hundred lives wandering just to be back here. Let us go and I will grant you mercy."

The werewolf lunged with inhuman speed, but Helesys was no mere mortal either. Her wand-arm found its mark before the matron was but halfway. An arcane pulse lit up the night and tore through the wolf's face and shoulder.

Matron Mildé howled and tumbled over Helesys in a pile of agony, gore, and rage. She spasmed on the sparse grass, half her face gone—white bone and a gush of red blood. Her arm had been torn off at the shoulder and lay smoldering in the middle of the group.

The druids shouted in anger, some of their faces already morphing as their elder's did. Their robes fell and dissolved into air.

With the matron's spell broken, Taunauk stepped forward with battleaxe in hand, but it was Helesys who spoke next.

"Be still and think! She lives," Helesys said, gesturing toward the writhing werewolf. She turned toward Qinmarïs. "What happens when you die?"

The druid's mouth was agape but he stuttered an answer. "We are reborn somewhere else... Hear me brothers and sisters! There is no need to die and to suffer the wandering again. Go to your mother and not to death."

Thankfully, Qinmarïs's words rang true and all but one of the druids reformed and went to their matron's side. The lone wolf snarled at them.

Helesys let lightning dance across her metal fingertips. "It would be an easy thing. A hundred lifetimes of suffering await you."

It was not her threat, but the hands of Qinmarïs upon the wolf's shoulders that stayed her. The young women reemerged in much the same gross transformation and whispered words to reconjure her cloak. Then she too went to the matron.

Qinmarïs grabbed Matron Mildé's robe from the dirt, walked over and draped it across his elder. She had reformed back to her thin, elvin figure and lay on the ground with her head on another's lap. Three of the druids said prayers over her wounds, cauterizing them with magic.

Taunauk put a hand on Helesys's shoulder and looked off to the woods. She nodded.

When the two had turned to go, the matron called out with ragged breath, "Vi neniam trovos hejmon!"

Helesys turned to see the maimed face of the elvin matron one last time. Another realization came to Helesys in that moment: That in another life, she would've killed the creature *and* the other druids out of spite. She felt this to be true, even though she did not remember having caused such violence. And it caused Helesys great shame that such a memory should return before that of her mother or father.

The elf weaver called back, "May you never know mercy again. Not even when you deserve it."

Then she and Taunauk left the wounded pack and ventured deeper into the endless gloom of the forest.

It wasn't until some hour later that Taunauk said, "Thank you."

"We each have our strengths. Think nothing of it."

"What did she say back there? Why did you curse her?"

Helesys stared off into the gloom. "She said that we will never find home."

~ ~ ~

The Road

A great expanse of the forest passed in respectful silence. Helesys felt like her gauntlet had been overcharged—except that it wasn't her arm that shook with power, but her own body with bottled anger. Taunauk must have been able to tell, for he was as silent as the great trees they walked between. Whether his powers of natural observation were merely due to him being in touch with his surroundings or from some outlander magic, she did not know.

Yet the silence had not been a solitude either, for Helesys's mind swirled with questions about the woman she was and how different she might now be.

Helesys knew that sparing Matron Mildé and sparing the other wolf-druids had been the *right* thing to do—that she would be wrong to needlessly damn others to the fate that her and Taunauk were bound. As despicable as the matron was, her and her villagers were home, and Helesys and her comrade were trespassing.

Still, she could not shake her recollection of the person she used to be: One of easy violence and retribution against the wolf-druids. The anger and violence she felt had to be turned somewhere, and so she turned it inward. Perhaps it too would maim her, like holding onto the arcane energy of her wand for too long.

Neither spoke until they came to a sprawling road. The cobblestone stretched fifty paces across in width and endlessly in length. It was here that Helesys and Taunauk saw two incredible sights—the true measure of where they were going and where they had been.

In their direction of travel, the road stretched off to the horizon and ended at an even more massive wall. The color of muted copper, the wall seemed to stretch up to the stars and as Helesys tried to imagine how tall it might have been, her breath caught in her throat, for they were still miles away. Even though she could only see a sliver of the wall between the canopies of great trees, she imagined it spanned an impossible distance around them.

"By Movernus," she whispered. "Taunauk…"

The elf turned and found her comrade in an equal stupor, except that he was looking back in the direction they came… Back toward the dungeon.

When they entered the forest, the dungeon had risen so high that she could not look upon it without nearly falling over.

Even now, even miles away from it, the dungeon stretched upward to ungodly heights. She craned her neck again to follow the stone until it became void-black and blotted out the stars. Like the wall, she could only see a sliver through the treetops, but even that was more than enough for Helesys.

With just a glimpse she had seen towers, peaks and spires. She had seen the bounds of the dungeon—seen that it was but a small part of an immense castle. Even the surrounding forest was staggering.

Again Helesys trembled and felt the quiet whisper: *You will never be free. You will always look back and see the towering darkness from over the trees.*

Yet in the overwhelming darkness of the wood, she felt a candle of hope within her for she had seen the limits of their ungodly world.

There was an end to their prison.

~

They walked through the treeline, parallel to the road. Taunauk had insisted though they both knew it would not help much for the trees were spaced far apart and it would be an easy thing to see them.

From behind them came the steady pounding of wagon wheels on the cobblestone road. Helesys and Taunauk stopped and hid behind one of the great trees until the wagon came close enough to see.

It was large, open-topped and pulled by two horses. There were five Terrans: Two women and three men, one of which was the driver. Weapons resting at their sides.

"Scouts," Taunauk whispered.

Helesys eyed their wagon again. It's sides were short and the people appeared to travel with no provisions besides themselves and their weapons.

"They look reasonable enough," she replied. But then, so had the druids. "What do your senses tell you?"

The barbarian shook his head. "I do not know."

"Follow my lead," she said.

When the wagon was thirty paces away, Helesys stepped out from the tree with her hands raised to her shoulders. "Salve viatores." Taunauk stepped out without saying a greeting.

Immediately the wagon halted and the people drew weapons, but the woman wearing a dark cloak over her shoulders raised a hand to stay them. The other woman was the last to lower her bow and only when her comrade laid a hand on her shoulder.

The wagon came within ten paces while the people looked upon Helesys and Taunauk with narrow eyes. The dark-cloaked woman stood, pulled back the hood and revealed flame-red hair and a strong face of youth. Her eyes began to glow a brilliant silver and when she spoke her voice overlapped with a man's, as if two were speaking through one mouth.

"*You who wander, state your intent.*"

"Safe passage." Helesys pointed toward the great wall in the distance. "We mean only to take hospitality and information, if you would have it."

The woman's eyes burned bright and she held their gaze for a long moment. Helesys felt something akin to scrying—something was watching them through the young woman's eyes. Being watched was an unnerving and paranoia-inducing feeling, but at least this time Helesys understood the trick.

Finally the woman said with voices, "*Weaver and outlander, we are but humble peasants in your midst. Danger comes in many forms in the Wode. You would be more a danger to us than we are to you.*"

"Is there nothing we can do to set you at ease?" Helesys asked.

"*Outlander, your people are honorable, yes?*"

"Yes."

"*Then make a vow to honor the wishes of our village, and in the same breath, protect us from the weaver.*"

Helesys recalled the words of Widewill, the goblin outcast, when he told her that weavers were not to be trusted. She smirked at the hypocrisy from the young woman with glowing eyes.

Taunauk answered with steady proclamation, "I shall honor my guests' house. I shall stay my own hand and the hand of those who travel with me."

"*Very well*," the young woman said. The glow in her eyes faded as did the second voice. "You may come with us."

~

Helesys and Taunauk rode with the villagers on the back of the wagon. In spite of Taunauk's vow, only the black-cloaked woman was at ease. The others kept a hand on sword or shield or bow, and even the driver glanced around nervously. They were all human, save for one of the men who was an elf.

When the weaver and barbarian offered their names, she was the only one that returned hers. She was Perdita.

"Odd that you would not trust a weaver," Helesys said, "when you yourself are one."

Perdita sat straight and rigid and replied, "I am a mere channeler. My power is given and may be taken at any time."

"Who gifted you?"

One of the elders, a man with a thin beard started to speak, but Perdita shot him a look that ceased him.

"I speak for the Deacon and he speaks for our god."

"A channeler of a channeler..." Helesys mused.

"More honest than a weaver. We must act in accordance with a creed. You have no such bearing."

Helesys tried not to scoff, but couldn't help herself. "I have no hidden motives. They are my own."

Perdita looked away from Helesys and eyed the floor of the wagon. "We are what we are. Do not forget your vow."

Taunauk grunted, "We will not."

Despite her comrade's sideways glance, Helesys already knew she had offended their host. The first humans and elves they come across and the weaver was already driving a wedge between them.

Helesys turned to the elven man across from her. His face was soft and filled with uncertainty. Young for an elf and old for a human.

"Are there other elves there?" Helesys asked.

He nodded slightly. "There is a mix… Have you seen no others?"

The weaver hesitated but hoped that honesty would suit her best. "Only the matron of the druids."

The wagon responded in a mix of emotion: Fear, worry, and anger. Perdita stayed them all with a hand.

"*Were you bitten?*" she asked, her eyes glowing silver again. Channeling the voice of the Deacon over hers.

"No," Helesys replied, "but not for their lack of trying."

"*Did you injure any of them?*"

"Only Matron Mildé. She lives, but I doubt they will ever show us hospitality again."

At that, Perdita erupted into cackling laughter, her voice completely overshadowed by the masculine rumble of the Deacon. "*Good. That bitch.*" When the horrid laughter finally subsided and the glow faded from her eyes, Perdita shuddered and pulled her knees to her chest.

After a moment, the elf responded, "Our village and the matron's pack live in balance, but it was not always so. Some of our dearest friends were taken in the night and were turned. We share the Deacon's sentiments about the wolf-mother but we wish no harm to our friends."

"None of your friends were harmed," Helesys replied.

The wagon looked to Taunauk. "The weaver speaks the truth."

~

Most of the rattling journey over the cobblestone took place in relative silence. Until they came to the woodsmen.

There were Terran shapes out in the gloom. Dozens of them dotted the treeline, steadily appearing closer and closer to the road. They were made of twisted branches and bark, with Terran faces. Perfectly still.

Helesys's wand arm hummed with power, with apprehension. Both her and Taunauk rose to a knee in anticipation.

"Do not be afraid," Perdita said with her own voice. She stood with arms extended to balance. The wagon never stopped. "They are dryads."

"Woodsmen," Taunauk added. "Men of birch and bark."

"They are a plague."

As Perdita said the words, the dryads came to life, moving in stuttering motion like the flicker of a flame in the dark. They strode toward the wagon, each as large as the barbarian.

Taunauk placed his giant shield between them and the dryads. It was so large that it covered nearly a third of the wagon. Helesys kindled the power of her arm, ready to strike.

"*There is no need*," Perdita said, her voice overlapping with the Deacon's voice. "*Siccum putredine.*" As they said the words, the dryads raised their bark-limbs and a hail of thorns shot forth, so dense it turned the black gloom of the forest a haze of grey.

But a wave of mist rolled out from the wagon, across the cobblestone and into the forest. As the hail of thorns passed into it, they floated to the ground and covered the road with ash and soot. The mist rolled further, shriveling the grass and blackening the bark of the trees.

And when it reached the woodsmen, they roared in a guttural, crackling language—the sound of trees breaking upon an animal's back. They too turned black and charred. Within seconds the forest was silent again, save for the wagon wheels upon the cobblestone. Pieces of dryad broke and crumbled to the ground.

The black rot crept up the giant trees but as their color changed, a wave of normal color passed behind it. As if the damage was being healed as quickly as it had been done.

Helesys committed the words of the blight-spell to memory. Her natural arcane blast was effective against most foes, but she had discovered its limits in the barracks against Zhug's metal men and against the Many-Handed Horror, Shomosk. If she could help it, Helesys would not be caught without a weapon.

"They will blow away in time," Perdita said as she sat again, voice returning to normal.

Taunauk asked, "Do you always pass the woodsmen?"

She nodded. "Every day we seek strangers upon the road and every day we are attacked by dryads. They… They are confused. They are forever away from the forest they knew and this one is only an illusion."

"I do not understand," Helesys said. "What do you mean this place is an illusion?"

"These impossible things are not real."

The elf across from her interjected, "They feel real enough. We suffer, we bleed, we die."

Perdita scoffed. "And we are reborn. That is not natural. Perhaps you have lived here in the Wode too long."

The man shrunk at the fact, but it kindled a question in Helesys.

"Where do so many of the woodsmen come from that you should kill them every day?"

"Do not weep for them," Perdita replied. "They grow out of a single dryad. Death for them is merely the pruning of the branch. They must be culled, lest they take over the forest."

"Did the Deacon tell you that?" As soon as Helesys asked the question she regretted it, for the red-haired Perdita shot her a look that could've wounded.

"My lips are my own, weaver. ...But yes, the Deacon told us that. He knows much and keeps us safe. He is the reason we're all still alive here."

~ ~ ~

The Village

When Helesys had lost track of time and was weary from scanning the treeline, the wagon veered off the cobblestone road and onto the dirt. They followed wagon tracks worn into the sparse grass and dirt by countless daily travels to the road.

"There," Perdita said, pointing off into the gloom. "Nearly home."

Helesys saw the bark first, a great toppled tree across the ground, but it did not stretch across the horizon as she imagined. Instead it was chopped short and each length acted as a wall-side around the village.

It was a marvel that one could fell such a tree, much less arrange it after it was on the ground. It would take hundreds of men, tools, and ingenuity—Helesys thought of the Deacon. Magic could do a great many things, things she had forgotten or perhaps never known that it could do. It must have been magic that moved the trees. As they approached the gate she was even more certain.

"There are no stumps," Helesys said aloud. "Where did the tree trunks come from?"

Perdita said solemnly. "Everything comes from the Deacon."

The tree trunk walls had been reinforced with dirt on the inside of the village, allowing men to stand and look out over the wall. They shouted for the gate to be lowered. The gate itself seemed to be made from planks rather than a single sheet of trunk. The top was lowered so that the wagon rolled across and into the village proper. It took five men to close it behind them.

Helesys was taken aback, for it did not fit within the world of the dungeon—the prison—that she knew. The houses were square and modest, built of normal wood and thatch for roofs. The houses were arranged in rows, with a torch-lined path that led all the way through the village. Gardens lined the backs of the houses up until the dirt slopes of the outer walls.

A quiet murmur swept over the village like mist at the arrival of Helesys and Taunauk. Men and women peered out through creaking doors with children peeking through spaces in between.

Another woman with flame-red hair came out from the nearest house. The resemblance was immediate. Perdita introduced them. The thin, older woman was her mother, Kara. She greeted them with bright eyes and hands clasped in front of her.

"We who have made our home in the Wode, greet you."

Perdita held up a hand. "It's okay, Mom. They will not be staying long." She eyed Helesys before excusing herself. Perdita walked off, across the village.

"Well, then," Kara said, "Won't you come inside and rest awhile at least?" She led them toward her house.

Helesys hesitated only briefly before her and Taunauk followed. She had nearly forgotten what it was to rest. Was it merely a pause—a prolonging of their struggle? Or was it a means of pacing themselves—of measuring strength and resolve against a journey that could stretch on and on?

The weaver sighed. Already she was weary.

Helesys paused at the door and turned to see where the channeler had gone. Across the village Perdita disappeared inside a tiny, dark hovel.

~

Inside, the house felt even more modest. It consisted of a single main room with a bedroom off to the right. At first glance the room could be confused for a closet. A short table sat in the back corner of the room, large enough only to hold a few equally small candles. Tiny wooden animal figurines sat in the pools of wax in between. Helesys couldn't decide if they were playing in the wax or slowly being smothered by it.

It was a humble place. It wasn't just the low ceiling, or the lack of tapestries or other decoration… Helesys searched her memory but could find nothing to compare it to. She could not remember her own home or family, and yet she felt almost claustrophobic and… lonely… in a way that she had not felt even in the dungeon—even though there were spaces just as confined.

Kara bade them sit. Taunauk sat immediately, rather than continuing to stoop under the low ceiling. It was a strange thing to see him sit in a chair that was too small for him and at a table that was much the same. He sat in a half-squat, feet close and knees high. Hands resting on his thighs and leaning forward, as if he might leap from the chair at any moment

Something inside Helesys would not allow her to sit. So she leaned against the wall, arms crossed.

Helesys eyed the bedroll and blankets in the corner of the room. Kara offered, "Mine are in the other room. Those are for you, if you stay. Most do. They only sleep on the floor for a while."

"And after, where do they go?"

"Well, we find a dwelling for them or the Deacon makes one for them."

That confirmed why there were no tree stumps outside the village. "Quite a feat," Helesys said.

Taunauk grunted at the elf and turned back to their host. "Quite a village."

Kara smiled. "It is, isn't it? We've made a home here, which is more can be said for the other realms. We're civilized here." The red-haired host eyed Helesys's metal hand. "Did… Did it hurt?"

Helesys eyed her gauntlet hand and shook her head. "I don't remember."

"You will," she replied. "Everyone remembers eventually."

"Would you humor us? What do you remember?" Taunauk asked. Both he and Helesys listened with curiosity.

Kara picked up a wooden horse from the table, freeing it from the wax, and turned it over in her hand while she talked. "I remember my home. It was a little thing, just like this." She eyed the walls of the house. "My father used to carve wooden animals. My mother would knit."

When Kara became wistful and did not continue, Helesys asked, "Do you remember how you came to be here in the dungeon—in the forest?"

The wistfulness left her eyes and Kara shivered. "I suppose that's the one thing that hasn't come back to me. I remember wandering into the woods. Walking deeper and deeper into the forest. I was close to something. I remember feeling scared—

feeling dread—that I was about to turn and see it. Or see it out of the corner of my eye. One moment I was there and the next I was here… It's like falling asleep, I suppose."

Kara chuckled hollow and shook her head. "Sometimes I wonder if I'm just really far from home. Wonder if my parents are out there in the forest waiting for me. But I know it's not true." She set the wooden horse back down in the center of the table with the other pieces and clasped her hands. "This is home now. No use thinking of it any other way."

Helesys nodded. She felt overcome by questions, paralyzed by them.

Taunauk broke the silence. "How long have you been here?"

"Long enough for Perdita to grow up, but not long enough to see a sunrise."

The weaver and barbarian shared a glance. "So long…" the outlander said.

Helesys said, "Someone else spoke of a sunrise. What's so important about it?"

Kara shrugged. "I don't rightly know. The Deacon is the only person I know that's ever seen the sun rise here in the forest. I never pried."

"Can we speak to the Deacon?"

Both Taunauk and Kara eyed the weaver now.

"We have so very many questions." Helesys returned Kara's stare in earnest. "Is it because I am a weaver?"

Their host glanced at the elf's arm. "It is not only because of that."

"Then it is the deacon."

"Have you ever been without your magic? Have you ever been powerless?"

The weaver shook her head. "Not that I can remember."

"Then you can't understand what it's like when us normal folk stand next to you or sit in the room with you. To know that you could destroy me in a thousand ways or make me think thoughts that aren't my own. But you might—you talk to the Deacon and you'll know what I mean. To stand next to someone who can work wonders, do things that are impossible.

"He made these," Kara pointed to the wooden animals. "Just like they were when I was a girl. Before I... He's given us a life here. Remember that when you talk to him."

The door creaked open and Perdita walked in. "Come with me." Then her eyes glowed with a gentle silver as the voice of the Deacon overlapped hers. "*I want to meet you.*"

~

They followed Perdita alone as the rest of the town watched.

The Deacon's house was at the end of the path—a tiny hovel that barely seemed enough for a goblin. Though the entire village was lit by torches, no torches were near the house. The wood itself even seemed to be a darker shade than the wood of the other homes. When they were close enough to touch, Helesys saw that its dark wood was covered in slanted runes of which she could only guess the meaning.

Perdita pushed the door open with eerie silence, revealing candlelight beyond, and ducked inside. Helesys and Taunauk followed.

The elf paused once inside, awestruck at the sight. The mere hovel that the dwelling appeared was anything but. On the inside, it opened up into a modest church, only a little wider than the stone hallways of the dungeon. The walkway was scarcely wide enough for two to stand abreast and the pews only wide enough for two to sit together. At the front was a pulpit and lectern.

A man in white robes knelt at the small altar in front of the pulpit, muttering a prayer. Perdita waited silently for the Deacon to finish, and so did the weaver and barbarian.

There were no windows in the modest church. Instead the walls were adorned with countless pink-flamed candles and the spaces in between were covered runes that matched those on the outside of the hovel. Some were etched into the wood while others were written in black chalk. Now in the candlelight, Helesys could see that they were sharp and angular, and in some places looked like they were the claw marks of an animal, rather than writing. She tried to imagine the language that the letters represented yet snarls and sneers came to mind.

A moment later, the Deacon stood and turned to face them, hands clasped in front of him—plain to see. His face was pronounced and yet soft, and Helesys found him beautiful for a human to the point of disarming.

But her wand-arm hummed with quiet resignation. She thought of Matron Mildé, who had looked enough like an elf. The Deacon was no Terran or werewolf.

The Deacon was something else entirely.

His smile was measured and he waved for Perdita to step aside. The red-haired woman stepped between a row of pews and kept her head bowed.

"It is not every day that someone is found wandering through the Wode," he said. Helesys found it strange not to hear his voice interwoven with the girl's. "Perdita tells me you aren't staying."

"No," Helesys replied. "Just long enough to rest. We are heading to the wall."

"Let me guess, you're under ten? Ten deaths, I mean."

The elf held up two fingers of her normal hand.

The Deacon perked up, brown eyes wide, "Ah… To be new again. I perished thirty-three times before I found the Wode. But that was many, many years ago. How does it compare to the other realms?"

Taunauk grunted, "It is dryer."

"More open," she added.

"I will wager that you found yourself in the drowned temple? Tell me, do the Mollunks still reign there?" When neither answered, the Deacon continued, "No matter. Time passes. Even in realms like the Wode that have never known the passage of day or night."

Helesys searched her memory of the flooded temple. She remembered the faeries and the stone sculptures… "Do you mean the clam-faced people?"

The Deacon nodded.

"We saw only old stone depictions of them. The place is ruled by fishmen."

The Deacon's face darkened in a chuckle, as if the light of the room was suddenly repelled from his face. "The fishmen were but slaves back then. Such is the slow march of change."

Helesys paused, both taken aback by the Deacon's fleeting change in appearance, but equally compelled by questions. "But how does that happen? How does anything change when death is not the end?"

"Now we speak in conjecture," the Deacon waved a hand for emphasis. "There are some that say that eventually a soul turns to dust just as a tissue and even bone dissolve beneath the ground. *I* know it to be something else.

"You see, there is a balance here just as there is in a forest or a pond—strange as that sounds. Just as there are a number of deer to support a wildcat and its cubs, here there is death and rebirth, but there are also *lingering deaths*."

"Yes, we know," Helesys said, "That which is dead but does not die."

The Deacon's face darkened again and stayed that way as he spoke, "So little fear from the one true damnation available to you. To succumb to a lingering death is to be reduced to a shell—a husk—to be worn by another. To see through your eyes and not be able to scream. To dissolve into hunger or rage and remember nothing of the Terran you once were. It is not a fate to be taken lightly."

"It doesn't feel like any fates are kind here," Helesys said. She eyed the Deacon. "Why help us? Why give us quarter and humor our questions?" Her voice nearly caught in her throat as she asked the question, but she had to know: What was the Deacon's game? What would he want in return?

The Deacon sighed and his face lightened and returned to normal. "Leave us." Perdita turned to leave without a glance to them or to the Deacon. A silence passed as he watched and waited for her to leave the room. "I entertain your questions because as comfortable as I am, I am bored. My people—"

"*Your* people?" The elf scoffed. Taunauk glared at her but she needed no reminder.

"I mean what I say," the Deacon continued, unperturbed. "My people are safe. Well cared-for to the point of complacency. They ceased asking questions years ago. Most of them have been here so long they don't remember their first deaths or how long they suffered before they found this place. They were too busy caring about survival and avoiding pain to trouble themselves with the grander picture."

The Deacon must have seen the challenge in her eyes because he continued.

"I wandered long and I have watched over this village for even longer. I am merely weary. An older soul than I look."

Again silence took hold of the moment, filling the void, and dragged on before anyone spoke.

"I fear I am beginning to forget," he said. "It is a slow thing to feel the creep of time, like stone weathering to dust. Ground to powder. There are whole worlds within this place that have been ground down and forgotten." The Deacon trailed off. The implication was clear. If whole worlds had been forgotten here, then so too would he.

The difference was that Helesys did not intend to stay.

"Qinmaris… One of the wolves said the sun rose once," she said. "Did you see it?"

"Twice," he replied, holding up two fingers for emphasis. "In a world of night and dusk, a sunrise is a cosmic event."

"What does it mean?" Taunauk asked.

"I do not know. I only know that I will be lucky to see another sunrise."

Helesys smirked, "You speak as if you do not have magic, as if you cannot work wonders."

"A few walls and made-things are but transmutation—parlor tricks." He waved a dismissive hand.

She stared at the Deacon and the question grew within her, festered in her stomach. The Deacon had made many things for the village and the scale of which finally dawned on Helesys. He had made a home for Kara. Remade wooden animals from her childhood. *Wonders*, Kara had said—not *magic*. The Deacon can work wonders.

The question slipped out. She had not meant to ask it, to give breath and life to it. But she could think of nothing else.

"What is Perdita?"

He answered plainly. "She is a citizen of our village. A channeler. She is Kara's own flesh and blood. She is a *made-thing*. Does this upset you, weaver?

"And what are *you*?"

"I am an old soul who can work wonders, yet who is trapped here the same as any other cowering Terran or crawling creature. I am a channeler of a god whose voice I have forgotten. My god has either forgotten about me or... even he cannot free me from this place."

The air hung heavy in the room and Taunauk turned to his comrade, no doubt feeling her unease.

The Deacon waved a hand. "You may go. Go and rest, but do not dawdle. It does not suit you, weaver. Nor you, outlander."

"No," Helesys replied, surprising even herself. "Not yet. I want to see. I want to see you do it."

The Deacon smiled now. "Normally, I would not share such a feat so soon, but your time is short. Wait outside. There will be a ceremony. I'm sure Maria and her beau will be pleased for their wait to be over."

He bid them stay in the village. Helesys shivered as the left the small hovel

~

There was a mound of earth behind the tree trunk wall that lined the village. The two sat on the top of the mound, and though they faced each other, they overlooked both the forest and the village. Neither content to focus on one over the other. Helesys leaned back on her hands while Taunauk sat cross-legged, hunched over in contemplation.

While they waited, they each went through their small equipment packs. They had been so set in escape that they had not thought to check what they had. Between the two of them they had four days' worth of rations, a waterskin each, fifty feet of rope, climbing pitons and bandages. Both the rope and pitons were covered in dust—already used. Taunauk's pack also had a crowbar.

Both the weaver and the outlander considered the loadout while it was spread on the ground between them.

The tools spoke plainly enough to her. "A dungeoneer's set. We knew where we were going or at least thought we did."

Taunauk grunted in affirmation. "Food for four days…"

"This place, wherever it is, is not far from civilization."

He nodded. "No traps. No bow for hunting."

Helesys stared at the sprawl of items and tried to suppress a shiver. It was eerie to see them and not have memories of using them.

"What of the Deacon?" she asked while they repacked the pouches.

"What of him?"

What do you make of his hold over the village?"

Taunauk grunted and waved his hand. "I think it is none of our concern."

"You feel it in the air, as do I. Something is not right here."

"What would you have them do? Should they live from one death to the next? No. This is a better fate than they could manage.

"I see fear in their eyes," Helesys said. "I see Perdita's eyes and they are not her own."

Taunauk's eyes were hard. "What other emotion would they have here?"

Helesys had no answer. More impossible questions in an impossible place.

Her eyes were drawn to a young woman walking across the courtyard. Walking toward the Deacon's unlit hovel. The village—the entire village—followed behind her. They congregated in the center of the courtyard.

Helesys felt compelled to stand. Something inside her worried for the girl and something else inside her, even louder—scratching and gnawing at her—was curious.

The elf walked down the earth mound and between the houses and stood at the edge of the villagers. Taunauk glanced between her and the scene, torn between his vow to watch her and his own curiosity.

It was deafeningly quiet in the village, so much so that when the woman went inside the Deacon's hovel, they heard the door creak shut behind her. Somewhere in the quiet, Helesys's heart was beating in her ears.

Then the villagers began to sing, low and solemn.

When we asked for light, you gave us light.
When we asked for strength, you lent your own.
When we asked for shelter, you made our village and our homes.
No matter what we asked, all you needed was our flesh and bone.

The villagers repeated the verse and from inside the hovel came a scream and a whimper—something that did not surprise nor stop their song—but made Helesys flinch. Grisly images flashed across her mind, images of the Deacon cutting and torturing her, and something told her that of all the things she imagined, the truth was worse.

Taunauk's hand on her shoulder brought her back to the moment, to the chanting and the courtyard. She was both thankful and annoyed. Helesys knew she was in control, yet she had missed that her arm was whirring in anticipation of violence.

Perdita skirted her way through the crowd and stood beside them.

"What manner of sacrifice did you just offer the Deacon?" Helesys asked quietly

Perdita glared at her. Her eyes a clear blue—her own color. "One that has been freely given."

The door to the Deacon's hovel creaked open and out walked the woman and the Deacon behind her. Her eyes and shirt were wet with tears. She held a cloth against her right side with both hands. Bright red blood seeped through the cloth and dripped down her dress. Her husband and a toddler waited for her at the front of the crowd.

Helesys felt both relief to see her alive, and revulsion at the size of the wound.

"See to her," the Deacon said. He wiped his lips. Then he stepped back and stood before the village. A hush fell over the crowd, quieting even the whimpering of the injured woman.

The Deacon stretched out his arms. His skin and clothes darkened as the torchlight shrank from him. His eyes glowed a brilliant silver and then he yawned, his red lips opening both wider and taller than should've been possible—to a grotesque width. Helesys's mind flashed to the large wound on the woman's side. And from the Deacon's mouth came a lump of bloody flesh which he caught in both hands. He cradled the lump and began to press into it, using his free hand like an artist would work clay. All the while his eyes were on the village, as if he did not need to see what he was doing, or as if something else was doing the Deacon's work. Meanwhile, his jaw and lips hung slack and half-open.

From behind the Deacon's arm, Helesys watched spell-bound as he shaped arms and legs, a body, a head, face and hair. And when he was finished, a baby cried.

It was the cry that seemed to signal the end, both to the village and to the Deacon. The silver glow of his eyes faded and his mouth closed and returned to normal. He walked up and presented the baby to the wounded mother and family while murmurs of thanks swept over the crowd.

Helesys heard the Deacon's words echo in her mind: *A made-thing*. Her and Perdita locked eyes and Helesys's stomach turned.

"Do you have something to say, weaver?" she asked.

Helesys shook her head. She stayed silent but could not hide the disgust that churned within her. What had they given up for this meager life? What had they done?

Even Taunauk was silent. He would not meet the eyes of the crowd.

The Deacon turned to the weaver, the outlander and his channeler. His white robes that had been immaculate moments before were now stained red—still slick with blood.

Words got the better of her. Helesys asked Perdita, "Is this how you want to live?" She asked out of morbid curiosity—because she did not know how to feel about it.

Perdita said nothing, but bowed away as the Deacon approached. The entire crowd was watching now, apprehension on their faces. *Fear and awe*, Helesys thought. *They* do *often go hand in hand.*

Helesys turned to the Deacon. "I see the way the villagers look at you. How quickly their wonder has turned to fear... Or rather, their fear has turned to wonder."

"They should be afraid of me." He said the words flatly, without malice or pride. "They have seen me work wonders and give them a life they could never have dreamed in such a place. They have seen me work horrors to keep them safe. They wonder each day if I will continue to honor the old arrangement or if I will lose myself in the feeding and rip one of them to shreds, or if one day I will simply vanish and leave them defenseless and alone. Years pass and nothing will assuage those fears."

Kara walked over and stood beside Perdita. Mother and daughter. Their beautiful red hair brought back that nauseating feeling.

"You're not the first to look at us so," Perdita said. She lifted her sleeve and presented her arm, revealing bite-mark scars much too wide to be human. The missing divots were nearly the size of Helesys's hand in some places, as if muscle and skin had been scooped out.

Several more of the townsfolk also beared their arms and sides, showing the same horrid scars. Others bowed their heads.

"We all pay with flesh," Perdita said. "In return we've gotten a village, houses, even children." She rolled down her sleeves. "There was a time when the realization made me feel hollow. I know it is strange, but it is a better alternative than endless death... Or to not live at all."

"Would you stay with us, weaver?" Kara asked. "Would you stay in the Deacon's place and keep our village safe?"

No, she would not stay. She would not resign herself to such a life.

In that moment, Helesys realized what it was that made her sick to look upon the village. It wasn't some sense of righteousness she felt. It wasn't the sacrifices the villagers made or the meager life they bound themselves to.

It was the Deacon, who had resigned himself to meager lordship. A man who wielded terrible power and could work wonders. It was Zhug with his treasure hoard and strength and cunning who skulked in the abandoned barracks. In spite of their powers, they were as much prisoners as the hydra or the fishmen, the goblins or the villagers. If beings such as they had given up escape from this place, then what did that bode for her and Taunauk?

Zhug said there were *gods* trapped here… Even gods could not escape. Whole civilizations were trapped, buried and forgotten here.

Helesys looked upon the village one last time. Upon the lost faces of the villagers, Kara and her made-thing daughter, and to the innocent-looking face of the Deacon. Most would not meet the weaver's eyes.

The elf put a hand on Perdita's shoulder, but could not bring herself to utter any words, not even the single blessing she could remember for these people would never wander from the Deacon's village.

~

In spite of her reservations, Helesys and Taunauk rested in the village. They retreated back to the mound of earth that butted up to the tree trunk wall. The contents of their packs were still scattered over the mound.

The pair stuffed their belongings back into the packs.

"Are you alright?" Taunauk asked.

Helesys shook her head. The futility of their endeavor was fresh in her mind. "How long will we endure, Taunauk?"

The barbarian paused and regarded her with stern eyes. "As long as it takes."

"Will we? When mortals and gods fare no differently, what hopes is there for us? The Deacon might have lived a thousand years and this is what he aspires to."

Against her better judgement, the weaver simmered at the one person that stayed with her. Her fists were clenched. She felt like her wand writ large across her body—bottled power desperate for release—and felt powerless in spite of it.

"You were silent in the village, Taunauk. Why did you not speak?"

"My words would not aid you."

"Even if you would've sided with the Deacon, I would've preferred your words. If we are to journey into oblivion and die and be reborn… If we are to survive, I must know where we stand."

The barbarian shook his head. "I feel conflicted as you do. There is no fault in the people's logic, nor in the Deacon's. Not all have our conviction."

Yet they had not met another soul who shared their longing either. She said, "To hear the denizens of this place talk, soon even *we* will not have such convictions about escape."

Taunauk's face grew serious. "Remember this, Helesys Byyra, *we are not like the others*. The gods and mortals are but slaves to the cycle of death and rebirth. They die and are reborn with nary their clothes. We can bring things back. The wolf-plate, Everfall, the magekiller token.

"Zhug hides because if he were to perish and be reborn elsewhere, his treasure would be forfeit. Zhug recognized this in us. Do not let yourself forget it. We will die, yes, but we will grow. And when we are strong enough we will wrench our freedom from this cursed place."

By the end, Helesys believed him. A half smile had grown on her face. "You sound sure for a man who does not know himself."

"...Things are returning."

"A copper piece for your thoughts."

It took a long moment before the outlander answered her. Helesys had been about to finish packing their things. Perhaps he had been debating staying silent again, or how to parse his thoughts.

"I do not feel that I have a village to return to."

"You are an outlander. Do they not live in villages?"

"I am Taunauk of clan Aonar. I remember now that Aonar means *alone* in the outlander tongue."

That had not been the answer Helesys suspected. Her friend was somber now. It was the same look of quiet desperation she had seen on the villagers' faces. As if the outlander realized something he could never have.

So quick their mood had swung.

"I remembered something else as well," Helesys said. "When the wolf-druids nearly attacked us, I thought of striking first. Mercy was... difficult. Violence seems to come easily as it did in the barracks against Zhug's goblins."

Taunauk regarded her. "But mercy was your first thought."

"Your words are kind, but that does not help."

The outlander spoke quietly, "Morality is a Terran concept. There are no morals in the lower animals. A wolf kills when it must. Other times the wolf threatens and postures. It spares other wolves to gain rank in the pack. They do not fight to injury or death—nothing that would make the pack weaker. That is all. Morality is a weight, a burden in an unmoral world."

"Did you always think as a wolf?"

"I think so. It is a familiar morality."

"I am not a wolf," she said.

"Nor I."

Helesys sighed. "I do not remember what I am… I fear that violence comes all too easy."

"You were a soldier. Just because violence defined you does not mean that it defines you *now*."

"That sounds like a philosophy, and we are ill prepared for it. You are an outlander and I can remember no philosophers or tenants."

Taunauk shook his head. "It is an easy question. A wounded animal is dangerous. What are memories but long wounds? A lifetime of pain or a lifetime of ease will turn the same creature into two different ones."

"You have negated your own argument."

"What of it?"

"I *could* be far different from the woman I used to be. Yet there is a chance that my memories will remake me. …I suspect that I would not have liked the woman that I was. I hope I'm wrong."

~ ~ ~

The Gatehouse

Kara bade them stay and rest a while longer. So the pair slept on the floor of their host's house and left in the morning, absent ceremony. It seemed the people of the village were not accustomed to people wanting to leave, nor were Helesys and Taunauk used to anyone wanting them to stay.

Then they set out upon the road, in the direction of the wall.

It felt as if they walked the road for days. The sun had risen only slightly, enough that the world was baked in a gray glow of dusk and no more. They stuck to the edge of the treeline. They stopped once to sleep and ate their rations sparingly. Neither felt like enough. Helesys's legs burned with a dull constant ache.

She kept telling herself, *just a little farther*, but it was a lie. She knew not how much farther they would walk but it was not *a little* farther. Though the wall seemed to both grow closer and grow higher in the sky, it still looked miles away. The impossible lengths and geometry of the dungeon hallway were writ large out here in the forest and on the road.

Helesys feared she was beginning to lose her vigilance. Long stretches passed where she did not take her eyes off the road and was hypnotized by the repeating cobblestone.

Thankfully, every time she looked to Taunauk, the barbarian was still as keen as an animal. It seemed there were no limits to his endurance or vigilance. She tried to imagine the life he led before: One of solitude in the fields or mountains that he scarcely remembered. Was it self-imposed or otherwise?

Helesys struck the thought from her mind, for if she had reservations about the person she was, then the outlander likely did too. How could she weigh either sins when they happened lifetimes ago?

Taunauk put an arm across her shoulders, stopping her forcibly. To their right were dozens of wooden people the same that had come upon them on the wagon to the village. The weaver peered through the treeline but could not count the eerie silhouettes that stretched back into the forest. There must have been hundreds of woodsmen.

Perdita—or the Deacon—had called them a plague. Perhaps they had been right.

"Do you remember the blight-words?" he whispered.

"Yes."

"We may need them."

Though their words were quiet, woodsmen began to stir. The treeline beyond writhed with uncountable men of bark and vine.

Helesys's wand-arm hummed with power, echoing what the weaver and outlander already knew. They would meet the mindless with swift and overpowering force.

"Get behind me," Taunauk said as he pulled the Ironwood shield from his back and crouched behind it. The dryads raised their limbs and the forest shimmered with a hail of thorns. The weaver ducked behind the fur of the barbarian's cloak.

"Foghar siorruidh!"

At the command, a veil of autumn leaves burst forth from the Everfall shield. They swirled and danced in a wall in front of them with hurricane speed, though Helesys felt only a breeze pass over them. The hail of thorns hit the wall of leaves with the sound of rain and where one thousand thorns would've struck, only ten hit Taunauk's shield.

When the sound of rain stopped, Helesys rose and peered through the veil of reds and yellows. The leaves parted as if by command and she fired a torrent of purple power. Blast after blast roared forth and tore through the woodsmen and blasting chunks of earth into the sky.

Through the woods and veil of autumn she saw countless woodsmen converging on them. Good. She would lure them close and then be done with it.

Taunauk pushed forward, crouch-walking behind the cover of Everfall until they were behind one of the giant trees. Their backs were to the road and it seemed as if no woodsmen came from across it. Even so, both the weaver and the outlander kept an eye on their flank.

Helesys shot from around the left side of the tree and Taunauk covered the right side with the magic of his shield. From their new cover, Helesys let forth her own hail. The blasts from her palm tore through countless woodsmen and sounded like a steady drum against the earth. The smell of charred wood and ash was overpowering.

The woodsmen were steady and slow and seemingly endless in their pursuit, but the weaver and her wand found a rhythm of death. The enemies of bark and vine needed little power to destroy and Helesys fell into a rhythm of destruction.

Thoughts of battle coalesced and a smile crept over her face. Easy, repeating destruction. Helesys knew that she was made for this—or her wand-arm was. Like a hammer being used to build, she—or her arm—was a tool being used as intended.

"Helesys, they are close!"

She turned and saw the heads of woodsmen just beyond the swirling leaves. Their faces wooden, frozen in blank expressions and the bark of their masks held together by green vines.

"Get Everfall away from the blast." The weaver stepped past the outlander, past his shield and the cover of red and yellow. The first woodsmen stood before her, close enough to touch. An army of bark and vine sprawled out beyond those.

Helesys raised her gauntlet and felt the familiar whir of power in its arcane workings—building, compounding, finally rattling in her arm. But this time the lightning that crackled between her fingertips was not purple but void-black. The color of death.

The closest woodsman reached out with a gnarled hand, which grew on vines, extending to try to reach her, but Helesys's words were quicker.

"*Siccum putredine.*"

Every other time Helesys charged the power of her wand, the recoil of the blast had blown her back, for even if the metal of her arm felt nigh-indestructible, she was still an elf of flesh and bone. No matter how she braced for it, the forces held in her wand were destructive even to her.

But not this time. When the words left her lips, mist burst forth from her hand like a dam ruptured. It was not a gentle rolling death as Perdita had conjured but a tidal wave.

Helesys expected the horrid, crackling scream of the woodsmen, but she heard only a crackling of branches as the mist blew through them and dropped them to heaps upon the ground. It was like they hadn't even had time to gasp as death overtook them.

The mist was gone within a moment, disappearing as quickly as it had appeared. It took only another moment for the army of woodsmen to hit the ground. The air of the forest turned black with ash and death.

The recoil hit Helesys. It crept up from her wand-arm, through her shoulder and neck to somewhere into her mind. She felt awash with regret and quiet despair. It sucked the strength from her legs as the magic had sucked the life from the woodsmen. Helesys collapsed to her knees and steadied herself with her hands. Her stomach wrenched and then she tasted bile as she spat on the ground.

"Oh, *stercus*," she said and shuddered as a chill rolled over her shoulders. "That wasn't pleasant."

Taunauk knelt beside her and put a hand upon her shoulder.

"Is Everfall alright?" she asked, hoping the terrible blast did not affect the Ironwood of the shield.

"I gave you a wide berth. Are you alright?"

"I think so. I had prepared for recoil, but it came in another form."

Taunauk did not ask further and offered a hand to pull the weaver up. Helesys looked out over the death and destruction she had wrought and felt somber. Somber that it had been so easy, in spite of the psychic blowback she had felt, and somber that the surrounding trees—the dungeon itself—was unaffected by such power.

"Do you see... What is that?" the barbarian asked. He pointed out with the blade of his axe, gesturing to a building deep in the forest. They might have walked past it if not for the woodsmen, yet it was only visible now that they had been reduced to ash.

"Let's see what we've uncovered," the weaver said.

~

The ruin of the woodsmen extended hundreds of feet into the forest. The pair walked through ash and broken dryads all the way to the ancient structure.

It was made from the same thick gray stone as the dungeon and was about two stories tall, mirroring the parapets of the dungeon on a much smaller scale. The part that was still standing might have been fifty paces square. The two windows Helesys could see were dark and showed no light from the inside.

Helesys looked back between the structure and the road and saw the occasional rock surface from beneath the sparse grass—perhaps remnants. Whatever the stone building had been, now it was half-destroyed.

As Helesys and Taunauk carefully rounded a corner, they saw small outcroppings of bark and vine arranged in a circle about a clearing. The outer edge bore similarities to the woodsmen in stature and figure, but they did not move at all. As Helesys looked inward at the circle she saw the figures shrink in stature and she realized that they were growing from the center of the clearing.

And in the center of the clearing and growth, she saw two statues in the grass. They saw the back of a kneeling soldier, the outline of a helm and shoulder pauldrons beneath a covering of green moss. In front of it, they saw the towering statue of a maiden, as tall as the gatehouse. In contrast, her stone was pearl-grey and no moss touched any of her.

Then the knight-statue stood up and calmly turned to face them.

There was a woman's face beneath the plate armor, seemingly half Terran and half woodsman, her armor a blend of steel and bark and moss. Her eyes were the color of moss and her left cheek was a sheet of bark.

"Long ago there was a Gatekeeper who lived here," the green knight said. Her voice was melodic as a song and carried a breeze with it. "She was raven-haired and fair. Ungodly beautiful and equally kind. She wanted for one thing, for someone to share her warmth... She waited long."

Tears ran down her bark-cheek. "I asked my lady for her hand, many worlds ago—for I could not stand to watch her so. I was declined and she accepted the hand of another. A wolf crest adorned his breastplate and magic covered the rest of him. They left the Wode, never to return. Left us lowly creatures with only fading memories of times inexorably forgot."

"That is a somber story," Taunauk said.

Helesys nodded, for she thought the same, but her gauntlet hummed ominously. She could not ignore it.

The green knight said, "I have never seen her again. I suspect they are somewhere in the castle walls, numb to the kingdom that has grown in their stead. This statue is all I have left of her."

"Perhaps they would know how to escape this place?" Helesys asked.

The knight stared back in confusion. "Death is the only escape."

"No. I mean escape from this prison, this dungeon... Back to the real world."

"I do not understand. Are there not stars in the sky? Do you not feel pain and warmth and loss and breath?"

Helesys glanced at Taunauk and saw his chest heave in a sigh. Was it possible to be here so long that they would not only remember their old lives but then forget them as well?

"You will wait here with me for the Gatekeeper's return." Wind whipped around the trees as she spoke. "You are in need of faith."

"You have enough company," the weaver said.

The knight glanced around as if she had forgotten the woodsmen and she smiled. "They are a blessing. They sprout so that no one in the Wode should ever be alone." Her moss-green eyes fell upon Helesys. "I *felt* what you did to them with the blight. Their deaths do not trouble me. Like lightning cleansing the underbrush. But their *pain* does trouble me."

"We will trouble you no further then. I will say a blessing for the forest on my way out," the weaver replied.

"No." The wind howled through the trees, amplifying the knight's voice. Helesys's wand-arm churned with power in response.

"Do not choose ruin," Taunauk said. At some point the barbarian had already drawn axe and shield in quiet resentment.

"Look upon you! You stand in my charge."

"We shall take our leave and we will go to the wall," Helesys called over the wind. "We have not forgotten the truth that this place is a prison."

The wind was now a storm and the green knight drew her longsword, a massive blade of shimmering green. In the span of a thunderclap she was upon them, as if she was moving with the speed of the wind. She swung for Helesys, but Taunauk met her steel with Everfall.

The weaver would've called upon the blight against the warrior but now she could not for the spell was so effective against the woodsmen that it might damage the outlander's Ironwood shield.

Helesys stayed behind the outlander, just as she had with the goblin leader Stizzai in the hallway of the barracks. The green knight's speed rivaled the goblin's. The ancient fighter was a whirlwind, a blur, a force of nature. The barbarian's strength and speed, though immense, would know limits. The knight's prowess was bolstered by magic and who knew how much she might draw from a forest so large. Again Helesys felt powerless beside the fighters—

—But she was not! The knight was a mage, one that Helesys should be able to counter with the magekiller token embedded in her metal arm.

Helesys called upon her arm, to the same innate knowledge that allowed her to conjure arcane blasts and warding light. Called upon it to negate the green knight's speed and the weaver felt the words come back to her.

"Lente et gravis."

Immediately, the stormwinds faded to breeze and the whirl of the green knight's blade slowed until it was no longer a blur. The ancient warrior was no longer a force of nature, but reduced to a mere mortal. And though the weaver's glimpses of the green knight were fleeting from behind the shield of the barbarian, the ancient warrior glared at Helesys—she knew.

Taunauk's speed overtook the warrior's. The barbarian bludgeoned her with the flat of his axe and with bashes from his shield, and for once he forced the green knight back. Husks of young woodsmen broke in her wake. Each blow sent her sliding across the grass and earth but the warrior never once lost her footing.

Helesys flanked to the side and fired blasts of arcane power at the knight, and it was her turn to keep the raging barbarian between them. The roaring purple bolts soared through more young woodsmen and off into the gloom of the forest to crash far away. The weaver cursed that she could not shoot around her ally.

Over the breeze came the knight's quiet voice, "*Freumhaichean de fiodha iarainn.*"

Taunauk brought his axe down in an overhead arc that looked as if it would shatter stone and the green knight raised her blade to block it. The two weapons collided with a clang of metal so loud that it rang through the trees and made Helesys wince.

The weaver thought for sure the green knight was split in two—that the clang had been a shattering of armor—but the warrior still stood defiantly with superhuman strength.

The green knight struck again and again, this time sending Taunauk sliding across the ground with each strike and yielding no ground with her blocks. Helesys saw a glow of magic at her feet, as if each step was anchored by roots as powerful as the great trees surrounding them.

She sent Taunauk skidding across the ground and turned toward Helesys. "I need no wind to best you, weaver. *Aon leis an talamh.*"

The green knight disappeared—

—and reappeared behind Taunauk. With a horrid howl of wind, she thrust the green blade through the barbarian's back. Taunauk growled in pain and rage, and swung back with his axe like a wounded animal, but she kicked him and pulled the blade from him with a sickening sound. Taunauk rolled a dozen paces across the ground. He stirred but did not rise—

—not before the green knight was upon Helesys, vanished and reappearing close enough to touch. Blade already slashing.

The weaver dove to the right and tumbled across the ground. Her arm crackled with power and she sent four rapid blasts hurtling toward her enemy in the midst of her tumble, but the green knight disappeared and reappeared even faster than Helesys could command her gauntlet. She did not have time to rise before the knight's blade was overhead and Helesys dove across the ground again.

The shout of the knight's voice came upon the breeze, "If you will not stand and face me then I will make you. *Greim oirre*," and before Helesys could fear their meaning, vines shot out of the ground and snared her arms, her legs, her body. They tightened and pulled her to the ground. Helesys was trapped on her knees and unable to move.

The green knight appeared once more, this time directly in front of her. "You are a crude and powerless lot." Her voice rose with the wind. "Have you anything to say before I send you? Do not plead for mercy for my blade is a falling oak."

Meanwhile, the weaver stared back defiantly, her wand-arm churning, building, compounding. Helesys knew not what it would take to kill the green knight, only that she *would* kill her.

"I have one thing to say… *Siccum putredine*." She turned her palm toward the knight. The crackle from her fingertips was short and the mist erupted in a blast as forceful as her arcane shot.

The green knight was hit so hard she was lifted up off her feet, torn from the earth and fell two paces away and on her back. She spasmed on the ground and gasped as if she was drowning.

Helesys felt the same pang of despair—the mental recoil from the spell—but this time she was ready and she did not care. She did not care what she had done to the knight. A blow dealt in defense and in retribution troubled her not.

As the knight writhed, the vines slackened and Helesys pulled free. She gave the fallen knight a wide berth and ran to her friend. Taunauk was kneeling, holding desperately onto his axe and using it to prop himself up.

"Let me see the wound." Helesys gently pulled aside the fur cloak and leather vest and saw the wound weeping steadily. Eerie green lines seemed to reach out from the wound and under his dark skin. Whatever sorcery was in the green knight's blade, it seemed to both be slowing the bleeding and growing within him.

"Can you stand?" She asked.

The barbarian nodded with short and sputtered breaths. She did not want to imagine the pain her comrade was in. Helesys stooped under his right arm and helped the barbarian to his feet.

She looked to the dark shelter of the gatehouse. She knew not what lay within but she hoped it was better than the gloom of the forest. "To the gatehouse. Perhaps something can be had in there."

Taunauk didn't reply and only shuffled forward with her. His weight was heavy upon her shoulders and she thanked whatever gods there were that he could still walk at all.

Their path took them close to the green knight, whose writhing had ceased. She lay upon the ground and curled into a ball. Armor crumbling to show a ragged tunic. Beneath the cracked helmet was bright blonde hair. The moss that covered her face was brown and drying and flaking off her skin. She was human.

The knight turned toward Helesys in anger. "What have you done to me?"

Helesys turned to Taunauk. "Can you hold yourself a moment?"

He nodded and steadied himself with both hands on his axe. "The blade holds the warrior as much as they hold the blade." It was a whisper, a prayer.

The elf went and knelt beside the fallen knight. Her wand-arm twitched with power, mirroring her twitch of anger.

Helesys said quietly, "It appears that I've destroyed your better half. Now, what have you done to my friend."

"You would ask this of me after you destroy my gift? Why should I help you?"

The weaver sighed and tried to still her anger, her quick-beating heart and her trembling elven hand. Her gauntlet did not tremble.

"You have been in this forest a long time, fallen knight. Perhaps you remember the world differently than I. Perhaps you remember a world of kindness, of chivalry and justice. I have no such fond memories. The more I remember, the more I do not like the woman that I was. She was cruel. If I were that woman, I would ask: Should I destroy the statue of your Gatekeeper, or should I burn you alive and send you wandering the realms? Both would be easy things. ...Do not make me be the woman that I once was."

The fallen knight looked away, and when she looked back the last of the brown moss crumbled from her eyes, revealing a brilliant blue. "Before I answer—how did you best me? Your arm was bound—How can you cast with words alone? You are no conjuror. You have no gift, no boon of power."

Helesys thought of the fishmen weavers who casted spells with words and staves. Zhug did the same. However, Perdita casted with words alone… It appeared Helesys could do the same, though she didn't know *how*.

"Did you think by binding my hands you would best me? I am no mere sorceress… but I have no answers for you. I remember little of what I was or my power."

The fallen knight nodded slightly and eyed the weaver's metal arm before answering. "My blade was fae-blessed, as was I." She looked to the silver sword half a dozen paces away. It reflected the star-light, completely clean of moss and magic. "Now we are powerless. Your friend's wound will creep and overcome him within hours."

The knight pointed to the half-grown woodsmen. Only a handful remained after their battle.

"A lingering death," Helesys mumbled.

"There is but one cure for him now."

The elf nearly grabbed her by the throat. "Tell me, fallen knight." But as soon as the words left her lips, she knew. She knew before the knight said the words.

"You must kill him. Do it before the green reaches his neck or it will be too late."

~

Helesys took the fallen knight's sword and helped her wounded comrade into the dark of the gatehouse. Neither spoke, but then neither needed to. Taunauk had heard the fallen knight's words.

Helesys would have to kill him and she did not want to think of it.

The inside of the gatehouse looked to be living quarters. There was a small wooden table and bench along the wall beneath one window and a wooden bed beneath the other. The inside of the gatehouse was pristine compared to the crumbling exterior—except for the thick layer of dust that covered everything. Light shone into the gatehouse from the two windows and cast it in a ghostly light. Small potted plants lined the mantle, a mix of greens and reds and yellows that Helesys couldn't guess the names of. Journals and torn pages were strewn about the table and most of the floor.

"To the table," Taunauk muttered. "I do not wish to lie down."

Helesys helped him sit and then looked upon his wound. "The green is spreading."

"How long?"

"An hour. Perhaps two."

"You heed the knight," Taunauk said sternly. "I will not become a mindless creature."

"I will, but not yet. You must carry yourself a little further."

Taunauk laughed and sputtered droplets of blood onto the pages strewn about the table. "Do not make me laugh. It is cruel."

"You are strong." Helesys ran her elven hand over the stubble of his scalp. It was the only fondness that she would allow.

She set the fallen knight's blade beside the barbarian and looked outside one last time to check on the knight herself. The now-powerless woman had reclaimed her spot kneeling in front of the Gatekeeper's statue, continuing her silent prayers. Helesys had ordered her to remain outside and so long as the knight kept her word, Helesys would not cause her further suffering. Regardless, the sight of the woman still caused Helesys to simmer with rage. She turned to the clutter of the table.

Parchment littered the table. Helesys looked over the sheets. There was writing—even some poetry—about the Gatekeeper. Most were incomplete.

When the sky was black and there was no moon, when the forest was full of saplings and the castle was merely a tomb, the gatekeeper's life was simple.

On another sheet: *And when the mistress tired of life, she gave herself to death and remade the world.*

On another she found the only complete verse:
What of you milady, lonely 'fore there was such thing as time,
Skin as fair as stone and heart the impenetrable same.
Your breast is the opposite of your realm:
You let no one in and in all other places, let no one out.

Another had versus remaining, yet the sheet was torn:
But as the forest grew and the stars and the moon grew full and bright, the gatekeeper's forest became full of passersby. Her village had grown into a kingdom...

Helesys read all these aloud to Taunauk. He was shaking now, eyes drooping and head nodding as he struggled to stay awake. The weaver checked his wounds and found the green had already spread from the wound to his chest—so much faster than she thought.

She had to muster her own strength to say the words, "It is dire. We cannot wait."

"Outside. Not here."

She took his arm across his shoulders and helped him stand. This time he leaned heavy on her shoulders and her legs burned. She wondered just how little strength and how much weight he had left. Whether he would so easily meet death if it was his last—if it was real-death.

They walked only ten paces onto the thin grass before Taunauk collapsed. The sudden weight brought Helesys to the ground. She rolled her friend over so that he could see the dim stars in the sky. Helesys felt cold in the open air.

She heard herself ask the words, but the weaver felt as if she was a shadow of things, things that had already happened. "Should I say a prayer for you?" It was a silly thing, for she could remember no prayers and no gods. Even Movernus, the name she had uttered in shock and in awe, was only that—a name.

The barbarian shook his head. His breathing was shallow and quick. "Be done with it. I will see you shortly."

Helesys knelt and put her metal hand upon his chest. The metal was an astonishing thing; it let her feel so much. She felt the churning of power, the compounding arcane energy. Felt the leather vest and the spasm of her friend's breathing. A crackle of power. A dull, wet thump and then it all fell away, leaving her hand alone—as if her friend had vanished.

She waited only a moment and when she heard no more breathing, the elf stood and did not look at him.

Across the clearing, the fallen knight watched from beside the statue of the Gatekeeper. She stood confidently, as if she was still clad in her armor, still blessed with power. A stark contrast to the fair woman she was.

Regardless, the weaver's wand-arm tingled with power, anger, and vengeance.

"How many deaths?" the knight asked.

"Three for him."

The fallen woman bowed her head in deep remembrance.

Helesys steeled herself and pointed with her real-arm toward the gatehouse. "Did you write any of those words?"

"Perhaps," she said, confused, "though I could not tell you which words were mine."

"You spoke of a knight. A knight with a wolf on his breast-plate that took your Gatekeeper's hand. If we cannot find another means of escape we will seek the knight and your Gatekeeper. Can you help us?"

She smirked, "You would ask a fallen knight of little memory where to find her maiden?"

"Yes. A woman with little mercy left asks this of you."

Again the human was lost in thought and her face began to wrinkle in sorrow. "I thought she would return but she never did. I… I do not know where to find milady for I never sought her. I was afraid to leave. Afraid to lose the little of her that I have left."

"Who then? Who would know?"

"One of the older souls. One of the wizards for they have their books to remember better than the rest of us. Seek them but do not expect their help either."

"Then they will find my mercy fleeting."

Helesys turned to look upon the face of her fallen comrade one last time but found him gone. Taunauk's body and weapons were no more. The grass where he laid was not even bent. She thought it fitting that their bodies did not linger after death.

"Have you no pity for us?" the knight asked. "We who have been here long? So long that we have both remembered and forgotten the people we once were. We that have forgotten our early deaths?"

The elf shook her head. She thought of druids that followed the wolf-mother and the villagers slaved to the Deacon. Of the fallen knight. "I have no pity for those that have lost their will. And no pity for the blind of faith. You swear to a lady who will never return to you. You have closed your eyes as you prayed and lost your life. I will do no such thing. I shall wander and question, and I shall do it with my eyes open."

Helesys turned and walked toward the wall.

The knight said just loud enough for her to hear, "May you find nothing but horrors."

This time, the weaver had no curse with which to reply, she had only a warning. "Do not follow me." Lightning crackled from her fingertips, an echo of her warning.

~ ~ ~

The Infinite Wall

The weaver walked for a long time and thankfully she walked in peace. She thought about many things.

The first was the fallen knight. Helesys kept looking over her shoulder, waiting for the powerless knight to seek vengeance, but she never did. Helesys walked alone through the forest and pondered what it would mean to have an enemy… One that would never stop, not even in death. Perhaps it would behoove her to be more kind than the woman she once was.

She thought of the Gatekeeper and the Wolf-Knight and though she had endless questions, the weaver had few answers. She knew from the writings in the Gatehouse that the Gatekeeper might have been the original ruler of this dungeon, for the writings referred to *the Gatekeeper's forest* and *her village*. That *she let no one out.* Stranger, that she *gave herself to death and remade the world.* But Helesys had no idea how much was true or merely the ramblings of a love-crazed knight.

Helesys cared only for escape. If they could not find another way, then they would seek the Gatekeeper and the Wolf-Knight.

Mostly, she thought of Taunauk. Silent, wise, ever-present… She had a fondness for him—that much she could not deny—and she spent much of her thoughts trying to figure out what it was she felt. The more she dwelt on it, the more she was sure that it was not romantic. It was merely a soldier's fondness for another. A shared desire to survive. To see no harm befall her comrade.

~

Helesys knew not how much time had passed, only that her legs were incredibly weary and her eyes were heavy with the need for sleep. Her wand-arm burned with a comfortable warmth and she realized in time that it was giving her body strength, like a well that she could call upon for nourishment. Her mind was a haze and yet she walked.

The wall grew large in her vision. It towered over her and she couldn't crane her neck to see the top. It blotted out the stars in the night sky.

It was only when she neared the wall that she began to worry about time. Though the night changed to a gray dusk and back again, time seemed to drag on. It felt as if the change of gray and black sky was a trick and that much more time passed than she thought. She began not just to think about Taunauk but to worry.

When they both perished at the will of the goblin-god Zhug, both had died at the same time and been reborn at the same time in the hallway. When Taunauk was slain by the hydra and Helesys crushed by the cave-in a minute later, both had been reborn at the same time in the hallway.

But they had never been apart for so long.

Had Helesys tempted fate by venturing onward after her friend's death? Would Taunauk be reborn first and be forced to wait for her? ...Would he wait?

Worse yet... Would they be reborn in different realms? Forever lost to one another?

The weaver thought these things as she walked the final distance to the wall. The trees disappeared behind her as if they were afraid to grow too close to the wall. Even the road crumbled within ten paces, and was grown over by green grass and dirt. From here she could see the wall was not sleek, but built of many arm-length stones. It reminded her of the rusted prison for the bricks were nearly the same color—muted copper or dried blood.

She walked the final breaths without stopping and then was close enough to touch. The stones were rough and pockmarked. There was no mortar between them—the gaps between the stones looked just big enough for handholds.

The weaver's heart was pounding in her throat. She reached out her elf-hand slowly, as if a sudden movement might bring down the wall or cause it to lash out and bite her. Even when her hand rested uneventfully on the stone her heart did not quiet.

In spite of her already aching legs, Helesys grabbed handholds on the stone and started to climb.

~

Helesys had no idea how far an elf could climb, but she surprised even herself. Up and up the wall. Handhold, step, handhold, step. That was her life and her every thought. She used up the climbing pitons early and left them behind. She made the mistake of looking down only once. Her eyes scanned the area between the next handhold and the next foot-hold—and that was it.

Now she was at the top of the trees. Her hands were cramping and caked with thin mud from the mix of sweat and stone-dust. Her legs shook with each step. The dull burn of her wand-arm—the only reason she'd walked and climbed so far as she had—was now scalding hot. Steam rose off the metal and it burned her skin and shoulder in the socket.

The wind whipped violently and the sky opened up into the deep black of night, and still she climbed. She muttered the words in a ritual rendered silent by the beastly wind.

"Handhold.

Step.

Handhold.

Step."

She looked up for the first time since her feet were on the ground and saw the infinite wall stretching up to ungodly heights. She could see only a sliver of sky above, for she could not bring herself to lean back—to chance falling.

Helesys fought the pit in her stomach and looked down—she had to know. She had to know what impotent progress she had made.

She saw the long way down. Hundreds or even a thousand paces down. Gods, how many hours had she been climbing? And she wept for it was a pittance compared to the height remaining. Tears whipped off her face and plummeted to the earth below.

The weaver grit her teeth and climbed further. Defiant against whatever gods or bastards were watching.

"Handhold.

Step.

Handhold.

Step."

A dozen paces later and her foot slipped, and it was nearly the end. The newfound strain on her hands made them nearly buckle and Helesys struggled to find her footing. Her whole body was shaking by the time she found a foothold and pulled herself close to the wall.

She would not make it. Not this time.

She would fall. She would find Taunauk. They would find a way out together. And if they could not, then they would find the Gatekeeper and her Wolf-Knight then wrest the answers from their throats.

Helesys turned on shaking limbs, looking once at the dungeon—the castle—her prison. From this height she should see it proper. It would be little more than a castle. She once thought the trees impossibly high and yet she had climbed the wall and bested the trees.

The weaver was confident she would see the top of the castle just as she now looked down on the tops of those formidable trees.

But when she turned her mouth hung open in horror.

The castle—the place she knew as a dungeon—rose upward. So very much higher than she thought possible. She craned her neck to follow the stone. Up. Up. The stone was void-black, like an abyss against the starry sky. It blotted them out and still it rose like a nightmare.

She heard *the words*. No longer a whisper, but a hiss in her ear.

You will never be free. You will always look back and see the towering darkness from over the trees.

The castle turned in her vision and it was a moment before Helesys realized—

—She was falling. Plummeting.

The castle—the dungeon—the nightmare disappeared behind the canopy of the forest. The starry sky with it. The wind grew to a roar.

"Not *this* time," the weaver said.

Then there was blackness. Silence.

And she thought it strange that the castle—the dungeon—was blacker than the sleep of death.

~ ~ ~

Reset Again

Helesys was falling again—

—except that her feet were suddenly beneath her. Disoriented, she hit the stone floor of the dungeon in a crouch, but instead of tucking gracefully into a roll, she collapsed and struck the floor hard. Her shoulder and ribs spiked with pain. She winced and forced herself to breathe.

She rolled over and looked to Taunauk... Where Taunauk should be.

All other deaths, the barbarian had appeared beside her, but this time the elf sat up on the cold stone and waited. Had she spent too long alive without him? Had her fears come to pass?

A pop of metal and stone scattering across the floor. Helesys turned and looked to the torch sconces that lined the right wall. Taunauk was there, pulling a torch free. She saw him renewed. He was no longer hunched in pain or sweating in death. He turned to her and stood with strength and quiet purpose. Vest mended. Again an outlander.

Relief washed over her and Helesys forgot about the quiet pain in her side. Her friend was okay. She rose and smiled wearily. Taunauk returned it.

"You're a few seconds late," he said. "Perhaps a minute. Was that all you could survive without me?"

It took her a moment to speak. "Hours… Days." She told him of the rest of the forest and her climb up the infinite wall. How she was so weary that her gauntlet gave her strength and how even that was not enough. She told him of the futility of that path, how the wall was impassable and how the castle rose up even higher.

The outlander listened thoughtfully. The graveness of their task softened his determination.

Helesys told him that they're task was to find the Gate-keeper and the Wolf-Knight. Her elven hand idly rubbed the plate with the wolf emblem. It was her one other constant companion. She felt that it was a key, but one whose purpose she did not know.

~ ~ ~

NEXT TIME ON
*A BATTLEAXE AND
A METAL ARM*
Book 4:

The Buried Hive
Available July 2021

Spoiler–Free excerpt from *BAMA 4*

Taunauk hunched over, stalking quietly forward. Over his head, Helesys saw that some yards away, the hallway disappeared into a void. As they approached, torchlight illuminated their surroundings. The world had not fallen away, merely the hallway. It was bisected by a giant borehole that cut across like a dry river.

"Does this seem familiar to you?" Helesys asked, already knowing the answer. Their first waking they had happened across the same--or very similar--landmark. It was their first introduction to the strange dangers that awaited them.

Taunauk grunted and pointed across to the blank dirt across the borehole. Where before they had scooted down and crossed the dirt to the other half of the hallway, now there was nothing but a few pieces of rubble.

"The hallway is no more," he said.

Helesys looked down the borehole. Before it had been impassable except for this small section. Now, the borehole to the left was clear and extended off into the gloom.

Taunauk grasped the torch with two spare fingers of his axehand, holding the massive weapon and the torch in the same hand. Then reached around the edge of the stone and brought back a clump of surrounding dirt. He rubbed it together and it fell away in chunks.

"Not so dry. Used recently," he whispered. He slid down from the hallway to the dirt floor of the cylinder in swift silence. Helesys followed and immediately felt the difference under her boots. The ground was spongy and the many fine rings that wrapped around the borehole were more pronounced.

"Fresh wormsign," Helesys mumbled.

"Yes. We will follow it." The barbarian pointed toward the open tunnel, the direction they were heading.

The weaver looked around and chuckled quietly. "I know we have no other option, but you make it sound like a *good* course of action."

Taunauk shrugged in the torchlight. "No other choice. Maybe worms can't turn around." Helesys did not laugh.

The outlander was right and yet some other worry tugged at Helesys. It was not an immediate danger, for her wand-arm was not burning with anticipation--a warning she had come to trust when her elven senses were not enough. This worry was instinctual, something deep within an elf's primal fears, something that even the wand couldn't understand.

As they walked on, Helesys judged the slope of the bore-hole... They were going deeper underground.

To be continued July 2021

Thank you for Reading

I hope you enjoyed reading this story as much as I enjoyed writing it.

If you did, I would massively appreciate a short review on Amazon or your favorite book website. Reviews are crucial for any author, and a starred review or even just a line or two can make a huge difference.

It's especially true for the start of a series. Thanks and I hope you enjoy the next one!

For a limited time: Sign up for Sam's *Monthly Newsletter* and get Free Phone and Desktop Backgrounds featuring art from *A Battleaxe and a Metal Arm*! Go to SamuelFlemingBooks.com to sign up, get some free digital art, and keep up with publishing and sales alerts.

Looking for more Bite–Sized Fantasy?

You might like **Tales from Another World, Volume 1**. The first installment contains stories about an undead sorcerer, a druid grove under attack, strange mermaids, a possessed church, a witch sentenced to burn, and commoners caught in-between.

The compilation contains the following stories ranging from 1,000 word short fiction to 5,000 word short stories:

1) The Final Ritual of Sircius Everdeath
2) Under the Waters of Digsonee Strait
3) On the Crimes of Hexing and Bewitchment
4) A Final Plea upon Still Waters
5) The Crypt of St. Lillian
6) The Blessing of the Autumn Herald
7) City of Embers

What to expect in
A Battleaxe and a
Metal Arm

I usually save this space for an "On Writing the story" section, but let's do things differently this time. So, what can you expect from this series?

1) You can expect a heaping dose of action, both of the battleaxe and magical prosthetic arm variety.
2) Expect to slowly learn more about Helesys and Taunauk as their memories come back.
3) Expect to learn more about the dungeon as our heroes explore its far reaches.
4) Lastly, you can expect a new story in the series every month. *Sword and Sorcery on a Schedule.*

I thought about going for a story every 2-3 weeks, but I wouldn't be able to keep that pace. I'd rather be consistent.

If you're interested, don't forget to check out the preorder link.

Connect with the Author

If you want to stay up to date on the latest about Samuel's publishing news and blog, check out his website and consider signing up for his monthly newsletter.

www.SamuelFlemingBooks.com

Samuel can also be found on Reddit, Goodreads and Facebook.

Samuel Fleming is a Science Fiction and Fantasy author.

He grew up in Maryland, spending most of his time swimming and writing. Swimming gave him a lot of time to daydream, so the two hobbies complemented each other well. Idle dray dreams turned into stories, some of which stuck with him for years. These days he swims a little less and writes a lot more.

He loves a good story no matter the medium: Books, TV, video games, comics, tabletop RPG's, or podcasts–most of which he attempts to share with his wife and three kids, and occasionally on his blog.

9 781954 679092